Libr

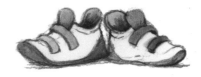

First published 2007 by Macmillan Children's Books
This edition published 2018 by Two Hoots
an imprint of Pan Macmillan
20 New Wharf Road, London N1 9RR
Associated companies throughout the world
www.panmacmillan.com

ISBN: 978-1-5098-4128-8

3 5 7 9 8 6 4 2

A CIP catalogue record for this book is available from the British Library.

Printed in China

The illustrations in this book were created using pencil and watercolour.

www.twohootsbooks.com

Monkey
and
Me

Emily Gravett

TWO HOOTS

Monkey and me,
Monkey and me,
Monkey and me,
We went to see,

We went to see some . . .

PENGUINS!

Monkey and me,

Monkey and me,

Monkey and me,

We went to see,

We went to see some . . .

KANGA

ROOS!

Monkey and me,
Monkey and me,
Monkey and me,
We went to see,

We went to see some . . .

BATS!

Monkey and me,
Monkey and me,
Monkey and me,
We went to see,

We went to see some . . .

ELEPHANTS!

Monkey and me,

Monkey and me,

Monkey and me,

We went to see,

We went to see some . . .

MON

KEYS!

Monkey . . . and . . . me,

Monkey . . . and . . . me,

Monkey . . . and . . . me,

We went . . .

. . . home for tea.

Monkey and Me
would like to say

Thank You

for reading our book.